Presented to

_____

With love from

_____

On

_____

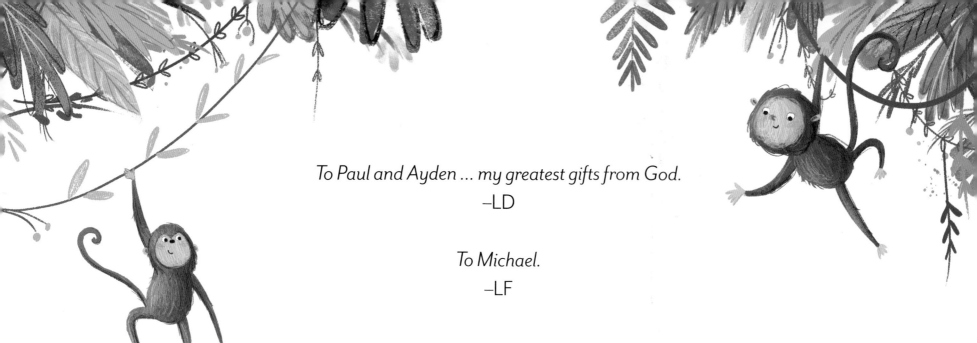

To Paul and Ayden ... my greatest gifts from God.
–LD

To Michael.
–LF

ZONDERKIDZ

The World is Awake
Copyright © 2018 by Linsey Davis
Illustrations © 2018 by Lucy Fleming

Requests for information should be addressed to:

Zonderkidz, 3900 Sparks Drive SE, Grand Rapids, Michigan 49546

ISBN 978-0-310-76203-4

Design: Kris Nelson/StoryLook Design

Printed in China

18 19 20 21 22 /DSC/ 21 20 19 18 17 16 15 14 13 12 11 10 9 8 7 6 5 4 3 2 1

The World is Awake

A celebration of everyday blessings

Written by

LINSEY DAVIS

with Joseph Bottum

Illustrated by Lucy Fleming

This is the day the Lord has made.
A butterfly floats through the sun and the shade,
while dragonflies flit past the flowers and trees
and grasshoppers hop in the soft morning breeze.

And the bees,
busy bees,
are buzzing today
as ladybugs call them to come out and play.

Just look at the sunrise that's painted the sky.

And look at the songbirds, all starting to fly.

The world is awake—it's a wonderful place,

alive with God's power and glad with His grace.

Out in the yard, just waiting today,
are all kinds of things that want us to play.

The gifts of the Lord are found everywhere,
and all that I see is just like a prayer.
So much of creation is happy and good.
Even the rocks would sing if they could!

It's in praise of the Lord that trees grow so tall,

that grass grows so green, and the flowers all call,

"Look at us! Look at us! God dressed us up too,

like great sweeping rainbows and skies wrapped in blue,

like water in sunshine and summer days too,

and you—beautiful, beautiful you."

And later today, what shall we do?
I know, I know! Let's go to the zoo!

We can buy a balloon
and meet a baboon.
We can look at the animals
all afternoon.

See that bear over there?
He's just trying to snooze
despite all the noise
from the young kangaroos.

The slippery otters are swimming along.

The playful coyotes are howling a song.

I love zebras and lions and elephants too,
pandas and penguins and owls that call hooo . . .

peacocks and panthers, a great mountain sheep,
and that grumpy old bear who is trying to sleep.

Down at the zoo, they're all on parade—

the wonderful creatures the good Lord has made.

My belly sounds like that bear when it growls.

It's time for supper, my tummy now howls.

So let's stop at the market for something to eat—
God always provides us
with wonderful treats.

At suppertime, I take my chair
and bow my head and say a prayer
to thank the Lord for all this food—
for carrots cooked and apples stewed,

for milk and juice and bread and cheese,
for even brussels sprouts and peas.
It tastes so good, I eat and then
I thank the Lord for food again.

And with my belly full, I start to yawn.
The light outside is almost gone.

Up in the trees, high in the leaves,
I hear God's love
in the sound of the breeze.

The wind is whispering stories tonight,
and far above,
the moon shines bright.

So I say my prayers and climb into bed,

then snuggle up close while my books are read.

The comforting night feels calm and deep—
calling me down to a dreamy sleep.
Calling me down to a dreamy sleep.

Calling me down
to dream
and sleep.